The Legend of
SLEEPY HOLLOW
& Rip Van Winkle

The Young Collector's
Illustrated Classics®

The Legend of
SLEEPY HOLLOW
& Rip Van Winkle

By
Washington Irving

Adapted by
Bryan Brown

Illustrated by
Nick Block

Cover art by
Jael

Contents

Chapter 1
A Sleepy Little Valley

*Found Among the Papers of
the Late Diedrich Knickerbocker*,
New York City, 1820.*

In the heart of New York's beautiful Hudson River Valley, right at that broadest place in the river that ancient Dutch sailors called the Tappan Zee, or "inland sea," there lies a small market town. Greensburgh is its actual name, but most people know it as Tarry Town. This

*A fictional character (a historian) created by Washington Irving.

name was given, we are told, in the former days by the good farmers' wives of the nearby countryside because their husbands tended to tarry, or linger, at the village tavern when they went into town with their wares on market day. That may or may not be the real story behind the name; I don't know. I mention it to be as precise as possible.

Not far from this village, perhaps about two miles away, there is a little valley, among high hills, that is one of the quietest places in the whole world. A small brook glides through it, making just enough of a murmur to lull one to sleep. The occasional whistle of a quail or tapping of a woodpecker is almost the only sound that ever

breaks in upon the great peacefulness there.

When I was just a boy, my first adventure in squirrel hunting was in that valley, in a grove of tall walnut trees. I wandered into it at noontime, when all nature is particularly quiet. The roar of my gun startled me as it broke the Sunday stillness. It seemed to last forever as it echoed angrily in the hills beyond.

If I should ever need a retreat, a place to hide from the hectic world and dream away the rest of a troubled life, I know of no better place than this little valley.

From the place's peacefulness and the character of its people—descendants of the old Dutch settlers—this lonely valley has taken its name: Sleepy Hollow. A dreamy spirit seems to hang over the land. Some people say that, once upon a time, the place was bewitched by a German doctor. Others claim that an old Indian chief, the medicine man of his tribe, held powwows there.

Whatever the case, the valley still has some kind of bewitching power that holds a spell over the minds of its good people. They are likely to hold the strangest beliefs, and have the oddest trances and visions. They are always "seeing things," or hearing music and voices in the air. The whole area abounds with wild stories, with haunted places and superstitions of the night. Nowhere else in the country, it seems, are nightmares happier to frolic through the imaginations of the people.

The main spirit that haunts this enchanted region—the commander-in-chief of ghosts, you might say—is the apparition of a man on horseback, without a head. Some people say it is the ghost of a Hessian soldier, whose head was carried away by a cannonball during a battle of the Revolutionary War. The country folk are forever seeing him hurrying along in the gloom of night, as if on the wings of the wind.

They report spying him on all the lonely roads of the area, and especially near the old Dutch church.

Indeed, some of the more reliable historians of those parts say that the body of the soldier is buried in that churchyard. His ghost continues to ride forth from the church in a nightly quest for his head! The rushing speed with which he passes through the Hollow, like a midnight blast, is due to his being late. Like all proper ghosts, he must get back to the churchyard before daybreak.

This is the legendary superstition, at least. It is the source for many a wild story in that valley, where the ghost is known at all the country firesides by the name of the Headless Horseman of Sleepy Hollow.

Another curious thing about this tendency to see visions and hear voices: It is not limited to people born in Sleepy Hollow. It seems to be absorbed by people who live there for just a short time.

No matter how wide awake they may be before they enter that sleepy region, they are sure to inhale the witching influence of the air. Soon their imaginations are working overtime, and they, too, are dreaming dreams and seeing ghosts.

Chapter 2
A Schoolmaster Named Crane

It was in this fascinating place, during a remote period of American history, where there lived a fellow named Ichabod Crane. Ichabod had moved to Sleepy Hollow to serve as the schoolmaster for the children of the area. He was a native of Connecticut, a state of the Union that is proud to supply the country with many kinds of pioneers. Every year, the state of Connecticut sends forth small armies of frontier woodsmen or country schoolteachers, like Ichabod Crane.

The name *Crane* certainly fit this fellow. He was tall and extremely thin, just like one of those big birds of the same name. He had very long arms and legs, and hands that dangled nearly a mile out of his shirt sleeves! The whole frame of his body was loosely hung together. His feet were big enough to be used as shovels. His ears were so huge, his nose so long and pointy, and his neck so skinny that his head looked like a weather vane perched on top of his body to tell which way the wind blew. If you saw him from a distance walking along on a windy day, with his clothes bagging and fluttering around him, you might have mistaken him for a scarecrow escaped from its cornfield.

Ichabod Crane's schoolhouse was a low building of one large room. It was made of logs, roughly put together. Some panes of its broken windows were

partly patched with pages of old books. It stood at a lonely but pleasant spot, just at the foot of a woody hill, with a brook running close by.

From this building, the low murmur of Ichabod Crane's pupils reciting their lessons might be heard on a drowsy summer's day. It was a pleasant, steady sound, like the hum of a beehive. It was not unusual, however, for this busy sound to be interrupted now and then.

The stern voice of the schoolmaster was well known in those parts. So was the sound of the schoolmaster's birch rod, as he "urged" a reluctant scholar along the path of knowledge. Indeed, this schoolmaster was serious about his teaching. He was a great believer in the golden rule, "Spare the rod, spoil the child." Ichabod Crane's students certainly were not spoiled.

Yet, he was not one of those cruel schoolmasters who enjoyed bullying his

SCHOOL RULES
1. Come to chum...
2. ...
3. ...
4. ...
5. ...

young students. Just the opposite. He gave out justice quite fairly. The timid boy who flinched at the very sight of the schoolmaster's rod would be treated with mercy. Of course, this meant a double dose of punishment for the rough and rowdy boy, who would sulk and squirm and refuse to repent.

Ichabod Crane called this treatment of his students "doing my duty by their parents." His other favorite saying on the subject was, "One day you will

remember this, young man, and thank me for it the rest of your life!" This was usually said when the subject of his justice was rubbing a warm spot on the seat of his pants.

But the schoolmaster was also a companion and playmate of the older boys. On holiday afternoons, he would also walk some of the younger ones home— especially those who had pretty sisters, or had mothers known to be good and generous cooks.

In fact, the teacher had to stay on good terms with all of his students. First, he made very little money from teaching. It was hardly enough to buy him his daily bread—for the schoolmaster was a huge eater. Although skinny, he had the appetite of an anaconda snake.

Also, he had no actual home. He stayed at the houses of the farmers whose children he taught, according to the country custom. He would live and eat with each family a week at a time. In this way, he made the rounds of the neighborhood, with all of his worldly possessions tied up in a cotton handkerchief.

Ichabod Crane was careful to not be a burden on these poor farmers. The country folk found the costs of keeping a school and feeding a schoolmaster very high. So he had ways of making himself useful. He would assist the farmers in the lighter labors of their farms. He helped them make hay, he mended fences, he took horses to water, he drove cows from pastures, and he cut wood for the winter fires.

Also, he was a different person when he stayed with the families. He did not act like the strict authority figure he was in his "kingdom" of the school. Instead, he became wonderfully gentle. He found favor in the eyes of the mothers by fussing over their children, particularly the youngest. Like the lion who laid down with the lamb, he would sometimes sit with a child on one knee, and rock a cradle with his foot for hours.

In addition to these many duties, he was the singing master of the neighborhood. It was a matter of great pride to him to take his place in front of the church choir on Sundays, with a group of chosen singers. There (at least in his own mind), the glory of his voice completely outshone the parson's. Certainly, his voice soared high above the rest of the congregation. To this day, certain quavering notes may be heard in the church, and as far away as the millpond, on a still Sunday morning— notes that people say must have come from the nose of Ichabod Crane.

By these kinds of makeshift methods— "by hook or by crook," you might say— the schoolteacher got along well enough. In fact, many of the country folk who knew him had no idea how hard he worked. They imagined that he must have had a pretty easy life of it.

A male schoolmaster was an important person to the ladies of a country neighborhood, such as this one. The women considered him to be a gentleman. They thought of him as vastly superior in taste and accomplishment to the rough, uneducated men of the area. Only the parson was held in higher esteem. In fact, the schoolmaster was likely to cause quite a stir any time he appeared at the tea table of a farmhouse. A vast number of cakes and sweets were apt to suddenly appear,

along with the family's best silver teapot.

Ichabod Crane was especially happy basking in the smiles of the country damsels. How he loved standing among them, chatting in the churchyard between services on Sundays! Or gathering grapes for them from the wild vines nearby. Or amusing them by reciting the epitaphs carved into the tombstones. Or leading a whole group of them along the banks of the millpond.

The bashful young farmers' sons were not so happy about this. While Ichabod amused the ladies, they hung back shyly, like country bumpkins. They could not compete with the school-master's style and way with words.

As I have said, the schoolmaster stayed at many farms. As he moved in this way, he took news from one house to another—like a kind of human news-paper. He was an excellent source of local gossip. This was another reason the farm ladies enjoyed his visits.

Ichabod was also thought of as a man of great learning. People said that he had read several books all the way through! The schoolmaster certainly considered himself an expert on a book by that famous Pilgrim preacher, Cotton Mather—a book called *History of New England Witchcraft*. Ichabod was full of frightening stories about witches, and most firmly believed in them.

You might say, then, that Ichabod Crane was an odd mixture of traits. He

was clever and practical, in a limited way. Yet he also was rather simple-minded, and eager to believe the most unbelievable tales. His appetite for the superstitious was extraordinary. No story was too wild for him to swallow.

Ichabod loved to stretch out on the bank of clover by the schoolhouse and read in the afternoons after school. He would lose himself in his favorite of Mather's dreadful tales of witches—until it was too dark to make out the words on the page.

But then he had to get to the farm-house where he was staying. This meant that he had to travel through the darkest part of the forest. Every sound of nature that he heard in the twilight would strain his overheated imagination. There was the moan of the whippoorwill, that most mournful of birds. There was the cry of the tree toad, warning of a storm. There was the fearful hoot of the screech owl or the sudden rustling of birds, frightened from their roost in the thicket of trees. Every sound frightened him.

Even the fireflies, which glowed most vividly in the darkest places, set his heart pounding—especially when a very bright one would suddenly stream across his path. If, by chance, a flying beetle hit him in the chest, the poor schoolmaster was almost ready to have a heart attack. He was certain that he had been touched by a witch!

On such occasions, Ichabod Crane's only defense—against evil spirits or his own imagination—was to sing hymns aloud as he walked. The good people of Sleepy Hollow, sitting on their porches after dinner, were often filled with wonder as they heard the voice of the schoolmaster floating in from the distant hill or along the darkened road.

You could say that the schoolmaster *enjoyed* being scared. He loved spending long winter evenings with the old Dutch wives in their farmhouses. The women would sit sewing by the fireplace while a row of apples roasted on the hearth. Ichabod would sit and listen to their strange tales of ghosts and goblins, of haunted fields and brooks, and haunted bridges and houses. Of course, there were always stories told of the famous Headless Horseman. The schoolmaster found these tales especially frightening.

In return, Ichabod Crane would delight the old wives with his stories of witchcraft. He spoke of strange omens foretold by comets and shooting stars.

He also startled them with the alarming fact that Earth turned all the way around in the sky. This meant that, half the time, they were all upside down!

As I say, the schoolmaster found much pleasure in all this. It was fun, cuddling by the crackling wood fire in a snug kitchen where no ghost dared to show its face. But such pleasure was had at a terrible price, because—eventually—he had to walk home, alone, in the dark.

Many fearful shapes and shadows followed his path in the eerie glow of a winter moon. He was terrified by the smallest things. A shrub covered with snow would suddenly appear at his side like a ghost! The schoolmaster shrank with fear even at the sound of his own footsteps. He did not dare to look back over his shoulder, terrified that he would find some ghoul chasing him.

A rushing blast of winter wind howling among the trees was the worst. This sound would fill poor Ichabod with despair. Each time, he was certain that he was about to come face to face with the famous Horseman of the Hollow, on his nightly search for his head!

Still, these were mere ghosts. They were phantoms of the mind that came and went with the night. Ichabod had seen a lot of them in his time. He had met the devil in many shapes. But daylight put an end to all these evils, no matter how bad. I think that the school-

teacher could have been perfectly happy if these works of the devil were all that he had to worry about. Unfortunately, however, his path was crossed by a being more troubling to him than ghosts, goblins, and the whole race of witches put together. That troublesome being was a woman.

Chapter 3
A Lovely Lady and a Man Called Bones

Ichabod had several musical students who came to him once a week for lessons. One of them was Katrina Van Tassel, the daughter and only child of a wealthy Dutch farmer of the area. Katrina was eighteen years old and blooming into womanhood. She was as ripe and rosy-cheeked as one of her father's peaches. Everyone in the countryside knew of her great beauty. She was famous, too, for what we might call her "great expectations." Katrina, like any other pretty daughter of a rich man, could expect to inherit a lot from life.

Also, she was a flirt. You could see this partly in the way that she dressed. She chose a mixture of old and modern fashions to highlight her charms. Katrina liked to wear a collection of pure gold jewelry that her great-great-grand-mother had brought over from Holland. She favored an old-fashioned cut of dress that called attention to her figure. Then there was Katrina's petticoat, which was very short, and allowed everyone to see the prettiest foot and ankle around.

Ichabod Crane had a soft and foolish heart toward the ladies. It is not at all surprising that such a temptation as Katrina would catch his eye. Then, as if she wasn't attractive enough, he saw her father's house!

Old Baltus Van Tassel, Katrina's father, was the perfect picture of a thriving,

happy, generous farmer. He rarely left his farm, or even thought about the world outside. He didn't need to. The world of his farm was snug, happy, and well taken care of.

Baltus Van Tassel was satisfied with his wealth, but not vain about it. He did not live in the grand style as many rich men do, but he did find great pleasure in the abundance of his farm.

The Van Tassel farm sat on the green,

fertile banks of the Hudson River. A great elm tree spread its broad branches over it. At the foot of the tree, a spring of the sweetest water bubbled up into a little well, then trickled away, sparkling through the grass, to a brook that flowed along, contentedly, among alders and dwarf willows.

Next to the farmhouse stood a vast barn—a barn big enough to be used as a church. The very windows of the barn seemed to be bursting with the treasures of the farm. The sound of wheat being threshed inside could be heard from morning to night. Birds—swallows and martins—skimmed about the eaves. Rows of pigeons stood on the roof, cooing and bowing in the sunshine. Below, pigs fattened for market grunted in the comfort of their pens, while troops of their suckling piglets wandered happily about.

A stately squadron of snowy geese flew into a nearby pond, with whole fleets of ducks. Armies of turkeys gobbled through the farmyard, while guinea hens fretted as they pecked and walked. Finally, in front of the barn door stood the gallant rooster, like the very model of a good husband, soldier, and gentleman. He flapped his wings and crowed with pride. He crowed again whenever he found some tasty treat, calling his hungry family to share it.

Ichabod Crane's mouth watered as he looked upon this scene and saw a great winter's feast! In his mind's eye, he pictured every pig on a plate, roasted with an apple in its mouth. He saw the pigeons snugly put to bed in a comfortable pie, tucked in with a blanket of crust, and imagined the geese swimming in their own gravy. The ducks in their dishes were snugly arranged in pairs, like married couples, in a nice onion sauce. Each turkey was tied up just so, with a necklace of sausages. To Ichabod, even the noble rooster himself was a meal, sprawling on his back in a side dish.

Then the spellbound schoolmaster gazed upon the paradise of Van Tassel's farm—the rolling meadows, the rich fields of wheat and corn, and the orchards bursting with fruit. His heart yearned for the beautiful young woman who would inherit this land, and his imagination began working overtime. His eyes turned into dollar signs. Just think of how much all this was worth, what he could sell it for! With that money, just think of how much land he could buy out West, and the huge houses he could build there!

In no time at all, the schoolmaster's busy imagination had already given him all of these things. A new daydream came to him. There was beautiful Katrina, his wife, sitting with a whole family of children on top of a wagon loaded with their many household possessions. Beside the wagon, on a grand,

prancing horse, was Ichabod Crane himself, husband and father, setting out for the frontier—Kentucky or Tennessee or who knew where.

When Ichabod entered the Van Tassel residence, the conquest of his heart was complete. It was a spacious farmhouse, in the old Dutch style. The eaves of the long, sloped roof formed an outside porch that could be closed in during the winter. This porch held a wondrous collection of

harnesses for the horses, and nets for fishing, and a great spinning wheel.

Inside the house itself, Ichabod's eyes were dazzled by a series of sights. Pewter cups were arranged in a long row on a long table. A bag stuffed with wool stood ready to be spun. Ears of Indian corn, and strings of apples and peaches and red peppers, hung along the walls like holiday decorations. The sturdy, claw-footed chairs and dark mahogany-wood tables were polished to a mirror-like shine. A corner cupboard, proudly left open, was lined with great treasures of old silver and priceless china plates.

From the moment Ichabod Crane saw these great wonders, he knew that he would not be able to rest until he had them. There was only one problem. How would he win the heart of the beautiful Katrina Van Tassel?

The schoolmaster realized that he had a few difficulties in reaching this goal. In fact, you might say that a knight of King

Arthur's realm had an easier time of it than our hero. After all, a knight only had to overcome giants and wizards and fire-breathing dragons and other easily beaten foes. He only had to force his way through gates of iron and walls of stone to reach the lady of his heart. These were things that a knight of old could do as smoothly as he would cut a piece of pie. Then, too, the ladies of those days were always grateful and generous with love for their knights.

Ichabod, on the other hand, had to win his way to the heart of a modern woman who knew her own worth, and loved to tease and flirt. Katrina could change her mind at the drop of a hat. That, plus her beauty, made strong men weak. The schoolteacher knew that he faced a dizzying maze, in which new difficulties and puzzling tests could appear at any moment.

At the same time, Ichabod had to overcome different kinds of foes in order to win her—not mythical enemies like dragons, but real ones of flesh and blood. These foes were the other young men of the Hollow. Katrina Van Tassel had many hopeful admirers who, as they saw it, jealously guarded every avenue to her heart. The young men were usually in fierce competition with one another to gain her attention. However, they also were ready to join together to fight off any new challenger from outside their group, if need be.

The most fearful of these young men of the Hollow was a burly, boastful, rough-and-tumble fellow named Brom Van Brunt. Brom was the hero of the countryside. Tales of his feats of strength were told far and wide. He was broad-shouldered and athletic, with short, curly black hair. He had a gruff but pleasant manner; he was both arrogant and fun. His thick shoulders and powerful arms had won him a popular nickname, used by everyone: Brom Bones.

What was Brom Bones *not* good at? He was famous for his superior horsemanship. He was first in all the foot races. He was stronger than any of the other

young men. He was so respected that he settled all disputes, and he gave his decision with such authority that no one questioned it.

Brom was always ready for anything, whether fighting or fun. Despite his roughness, he was actually a good-humored fellow. He had more mischief than evil in his personality. Brom had three or four close friends who saw him as their model. With these friends, he would travel the countryside, seeking out every scene of feud or merriment for miles around.

In cold weather, Brom always wore a distinctive fur hat with a dashing fox's tail in back. The folks of the countryside would sometimes see the top of this hat at a distance, whisking along in the midst of a group of galloping horsemen. They knew this meant that Brom was on his way, and a big uproar of some sort was sure to follow.

Sometimes, Brom and his fellows

would be heard dashing along past the farmhouses at midnight, with whoops and hollers, like a troop of Russian Cossacks. The old women, startled out of their sleep, would listen for a moment

until the hurry-scurry had clattered by, then exclaim, "Ay, there goes Brom Bones and his gang!" Whenever any prank or fist fight occurred in the area, they always shook their heads and declared, "That Brom Bones must be at the bottom of it."

This rough-and-rowdy hero had been courting the dainty Katrina for some time. Brom's style of "courtship" might be compared to the gentle caresses of a bear. Yet, Katrina did not discourage his hopes. Also, the very fact that he was interested in her was enough to warn off any other rivals. After all, who would want to cross a lion during his hunt? Brom's horse could often be seen at the Van Tassel house on a Sunday night—a sure sign that he was courting, or "sparking," within. All the other young men would pass by in despair at this sight, and search for other more "win-able" battles to fight.

Brom Bones, then, was the dragon

that Ichabod Crane would have to fight for the hand of the fair Katrina. Many men stronger than the schoolmaster would have given up on that contest at the beginning. Certainly, a *wiser* man would have. But Ichabod Crane had a personality that was as flexible as it was surprisingly sturdy. You might be able to bend him easily, but you couldn't break him. Just like a tough little tree, one moment you might have him completely doubled over, but as soon as you let go—*sproing!*—he would be standing again, straight and tall as ever.

Still, it would have been madness for the schoolmaster to openly compete with Brom Bones. Brom was not a man to be easily defeated, any more than that fearsome Greek warrior Achilles. Ichabod, therefore, had to make his advances to the heiress Katrina in quiet ways.

For instance, Ichabod was able to visit the Van Tassel farmhouse frequently as Katrina's music teacher. Fortunately, he did not have to worry about nosy parents, as most suitors do. Baltus Van Tassel loved his daughter even better than his pipe, and always let her do whatever she pleased. Mrs. Van Tassel, too, did not interfere. As she would wisely say, "Ducks and geese are foolish things, and must be looked after, but girls can take care of themselves." Katrina's mother was a busy woman, anyway. She was always bustling about the house, or attacking her spinning wheel. Meanwhile, old Balt would sit quietly on the porch, smoking his pipe and gazing on the adventures of the weather vane on top of the barn.

So the schoolmaster was free to court young Katrina at his own pace. They sat under the shadow of the great elm for hours. Sometimes he could even be found strolling along with his lady at twilight, that hour of the day in which a young man's words of love become especially expressive.

I cannot claim to know the secret of how a woman's heart is won. To me, the ways of women have always been a great mystery. Some of them seem to have only one weak point, or door, to their hearts. Others seem to have a thousand doors, and they may be captured in a thousand ways. It certainly takes great skill for any man to win the heart of any woman. But it is the sign of a true general when a man can take and hold the heart with a thousand vulnerable points. To keep this kind of fortress safe, a man must battle at every door and window!

I say this with admiration: The man who wins many hearts is worthy of some kind of fame. But the man who conquers and keeps the heart of a flirt like Katrina Van Tassel is a true hero.

Brom did not act heroic in this way at first. In fact, he seemed to withdraw from the field of battle when Ichabod Crane made his interest in Katrina known. His horse was no longer seen at the Van Tassel house on Sunday nights. But he had not given up. Soon, in fact, it was clear that there was a deadly feud between Brom Bones and the schoolmaster of Sleepy Hollow.

Brom had a rough, old-fashioned sense of manhood and chivalry. If he'd had his way, he would have fought for the heart of the lady the same way those noble knights of legend did—in hand-to-hand combat. Ichabod, however, was too aware of his rival's superior strength to let that happen. "I will double the schoolmaster up, and lay him on a shelf of his own schoolhouse!" he once overheard Bones boast. Needless to say, Ichabod did not want to give him an opportunity to do so.

The schoolmaster's refusal to do battle in the traditional way made Brom Bones even more angry. It forced him to resort to—what shall we call them?—let's say the "special tricks" that a smart country lad had at his disposal. Unable to use his fists, Brom's chief tactic was to make fun of the schoolmaster, and to play rude practical jokes on him.

Ichabod became the favorite target of torment by Brom and his gang of rough riders. They made Ichabod's formerly peaceful life a nightmare. First they smoked out his schoolhouse by plugging up the chimney. Then they broke in at night and turned all the desks and chairs topsy-turvy. The poor schoolmaster began to think that all the witches in the country were holding their meetings there!

Most damaging of all, Brom took every chance he had to belittle poor Ichabod in front of Katrina. He even taught a dog to whine in a ridiculous manner, and then suggested to her that the dog would make a better singing teacher than the schoolmaster!

Things went on this way for quite a while. The battle continued without either Ichabod or Brom winning a clear advantage.

Chapter 4
High Hopes and Spooky Stories

Then came one fine fall day. The schoolmaster was sitting in a thoughtful mood on his "throne"—that is, the high stool from which he watched his students, the "subjects" of his little kingdom. In his hand, he swayed a wooden ruler like a king's scepter. The birch rod of justice hung on the wall behind the "throne," a constant threat to evil-doers. On the desk in front of him sat the many forbidden toys and weapons that he had taken from his unruly boys: half-munched apples, popguns, spinning tops, rubber bands, and a whole arsenal of paper missiles.

The birch rod had been used quite recently, so some students were staring at their books with an unnatural concentration. Others were whispering behind their books with a wary eye on the schoolmaster. A kind of buzzing stillness reigned throughout the schoolroom.

Suddenly, the silence was broken by the arrival of a messenger, who came clattering up to the school door. This was a strange-looking fellow. He wore a curious, round fragment of a hat that resembled the winged cap of the Roman god Mercury. His faithful steed was a ragged, half-wild colt, which he rode with a halter made of a piece of rope. His announcement was delivered with the kind of fancy language that some people are likely to use on such occasions. He was pleased, said the little man, to invite

Master Crane to a quilting party, to be held that evening at the Van Tassel residence. With that, he turned, got back on his horse, and scampered away up the hollow, full of the importance and hurry of his mission.

Bustle and hubbub now filled the schoolroom. Ichabod hurried his scholars through their lessons, without bothering with many of the smaller details. The smarter children were able to skip

over nearly half of their studies. The slower ones were given a smart hurry-upper in the rear by the schoolmaster's ruler, to help them over long words. Afterward, the students were allowed to fling their books aside, without putting them away on the shelves. Inkwells were hastily overturned and benches thrown down. The whole school was turned loose an hour before the usual time. They burst forth like an army of mischievous little devils, yelling and jumping about the schoolyard, in joy at their early freedom.

The eager Ichabod now spent an extra half hour, at least, preparing himself. He carefully brushed off his best suit—actually, his only suit—and fixed his hair in front of the piece of broken mirror that hung up in the schoolhouse. Last, in order to present himself in style, as a true gentleman, he borrowed a horse from the farmer he was staying with—an ill-tempered old man named

Hans Van Ripper. Finally, Ichabod rode forth gallantly on his horse, like a knight of old in quest of adventure.

It is proper that I, in the true spirit of this romantic story, spend some time describing my hero and his steed.

The animal that Ichabod rode was a broken-down plow horse that was very old and very nasty. He was thin and shaggy, and his mane and tail were tangled and knotted with burrs. One eye had lost its pupil, and the other was misted over with age. Still, the horse must have had some fire in his youth, if we are to judge by his name: Gunpowder. In fact, this animal had once been the favorite horse of the grouchy Van Ripper, who was as unpleasant a rider as he was a person. The personality of the master had obviously been picked up by his horse.

Ichabod looked as odd as his horse. For one thing, Ichabod rode with very short stirrups. This brought the knees of his long legs up nearly to his waist. His sharp elbows stuck way out, like a grasshopper's. As the horse jogged down the trail, the motion of those elbows, up and down, looked like a pair of wings flapping! A small wool hat rested almost on the top of his nose, since he didn't have much of a forehead. As for the tails of Ichabod's black coat, they fluttered out behind him in the breeze, almost reaching the horse's own tail.

Such was the appearance of the schoolmaster and his steed as they shuffled out of the gate of Hans Van Ripper's stable. Together, they were as strange a sight as anyone could expect to see in broad daylight.

It was, as I have said, a fine early-autumn day. The sky was clear and serene, and nature wore her finest rich and golden apparel. The forests had put on their sober brown and yellow. The first leaves of fall had begun to turn, dyed by frost into brilliant oranges, purples, and

scarlets. Flocks of wild ducks began to make their appearance high in the air. The bark of the squirrel could be heard from the groves of beech and hickory nuts, while the whistle of the quail sang out from the neighboring wheat field.

The small birds were having their farewell banquets before heading south for the winter. In a cheerful mood, they fluttered, chirping and frolicking, from bush to bush and tree to tree.

Ichabod jogged slowly on his way. His eye, guided as always by his appetite, took in the many treasures of jolly autumn with delight. On all sides, he saw vast stores of apples. Some hung in abundance from the trees. Others had already been gathered into baskets and barrels for the market, or heaped in huge piles for the cider press. Farther on, he saw great fields of corn, with golden ears peeping from their leafy covers and turning, in his mind's eye, into cakes and puddings.

Beneath the stalks of corn lay the yellow pumpkins, which turned up their fair, round bellies to the sun and promised to become the richest of pies. Close by, the schoolmaster passed fragrant fields of buckwheat, and breathed the sweet smell of the beehive. A sudden fantasy stole over his mind—of a small mountain of pancakes, dripping with butter and honey, made by the delicate little hand of Katrina Van Tassel.

The schoolmaster fed his imagination with these sweet and sugary thoughts as he rode. His journey took him along a path that looks out over some of the most beautiful parts of the mighty Hudson River. The wide expanse of the Tappan Zee lay motionless and glassy below him. Here and there, a gentle wave rippled the blue shadow of the distant mountain. A few amber clouds floated in the sky, without a breath of wind to move them.

The golden disk of the sun wheeled

slowly down into the west. A slanting ray of late-afternoon sunlight lingered on the wooded cliffs that hung over the river, highlighting the dark-gray and purple of the rocky cliff sides. In the distance, a boat drifted lazily along with the tide, its sail hanging quietly against the mast. The reflection of the sky gleaming on the still water made it seem almost as if the boat was hanging in mid-air.

Toward evening, Ichabod arrived at the Van Tassel farm. Many of the good folk of the countryside were already there. The old farmers were there—a thin, leather-faced bunch. They were all dressed in the old Dutch way, with homemade coats and pants, high blue stockings, and sturdy shoes with large, pewter buckles. Near the farmers stood their energetic wives, dressed in their matronly caps and homespun petticoats. The pretty young daughters were dressed almost as "country" as their mothers. Only the occasional straw hat, colorful ribbon, or white frock hinted at modern, "city" fashion among the girls.

Then there were the boys. They stood together in their identical coats with the short, square tails in back and rows of huge brass buttons in front. Most of them wore their hair in a fashionable kind of pigtail—especially if they were able to get hold of some eel oil, which was said to nourish and strengthen the hair.

In the very center of this group, the hero of the scene was Brom Bones. He had arrived dramatically on his favorite horse, Daredevil. It was a good name for this creature! Daredevil was high-spirited and full of mischief, like his master. No one but Brom could handle him. Brom preferred horses like this, which kept a rider constantly fearful of breaking his neck. As far as Brom was concerned, a horse that was too easy to handle was simply unworthy of a person of spirit such as himself.

Finally, the schoolmaster entered. Allow me to pause for a moment to speak of his first sight of the Van Tassel parlor. What a vision of delight burst upon his gaze! I speak not of the lovely young ladies of the Hollow, gathered together in a colorful display of red and white. The object of Ichabod's fascination was something much closer to his heart—the mountain of food on Mrs. Van Tassel's tea table.

Let's begin with the many plates piled high with cakes and sweets. There were too many types to even list! There was the hearty doughnut and the crisp and crumbling cruller. There were sweet cakes and shortcakes, ginger cakes and honey cakes, and the whole family of cakes. There were apple pies and peach pies and pumpkin pies. There were delicious dishes of preserved plums, peaches, pears, and quinces. This is not to mention

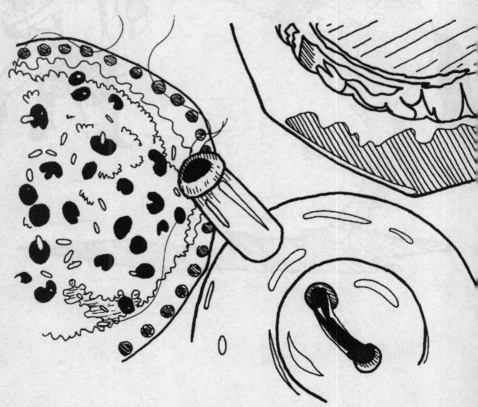

broiled fish and roasted chickens and slices of ham and smoked beef, together with bowls of milk and cream. All these treats were all mingled together, in one wonderful sight, with a motherly teapot standing in the midst of them, sending up its clouds of steam.

Heaven mark the spot! I don't have time to give this banquet the attention it deserves, and am too eager to get on with my story. Ichabod Crane was not in

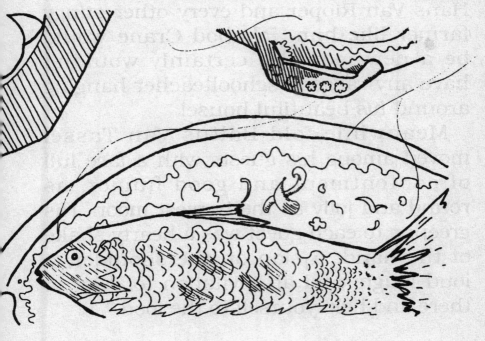

such a hurry, though. He took the time to linger over every treat on the table.

The schoolmaster was truly a grateful man. Indeed, his heart grew larger as his skin was flushed with good cheer. Ichabod kept rolling his large eyes around the Van Tassel house as he ate and chuckled to himself. All this could one day be his! He imagined how quickly his life would change. First, good-bye to the schoolhouse. Second, good-bye to Hans Van Ripper and every other stingy farmer like him. Ichabod Crane would be a new man. He certainly wouldn't have any raggedy schoolteacher hanging around *his* beautiful house!

Meanwhile, old Baltus Van Tassel moved among his guests with a face full of contentment and good humor, as round and jolly as the harvest moon. His greeting to each guest was a hearty shake of the hand, a slap on the shoulder, a loud laugh, and an invitation to, "Get in there and help yourself to the food."

Then the sound of the music from the common room called everyone in to the dance. The musician was an old, gray-headed fellow who had been the traveling orchestra of the countryside for more than half a century. His violin was as old and battered as himself. Most of the time, he just scraped away on two or three strings. His old head waved to the movement of his bow, or bowed almost to the ground whenever a new couple entered the dance floor.

Ichabod prided himself upon his dancing as much as his singing powers. Indeed, not an inch of his body was idle. He was a sight to behold—those long arms and legs in full motion. To see him clattering about the room, you would have thought that Saint Vitus himself, the patron saint of dance, had taken shape before you in person.

And so the schoolteacher, who had spent his day punishing schoolboys, was now the happiest man in the valley

that same night. How could he *not* be? The lady of his heart, Katrina Van Tassel, was at his side. She danced every dance with him, and smiled in silent encouragement each time that Ichabod made eyes at her.

Meanwhile, Brom Bones sat brooding by himself in one corner, suffering from love and jealousy.

When the dance came to an end, Ichabod joined Baltus Van Tassel and a group of the older folks. They sat at one end of the porch, gossiping and trading tales about the war of independence from England. This area of the country was famous for its stories of great battles and great men. The British and American troop lines had both run near there. Villages had been raided many times by armies. There had been a good number of refugees and adventurers, and many acts of bravery.

The old folks had lived through all these things. A number of years had passed since then, however. Perhaps the old folks' memory was not as good as it once was. Perhaps each storyteller took a little creative license to dress up his tale. It was odd that each one remembered himself as the hero of every daring deed.

There was the story of Doffue Martling, a large, blue-bearded Dutchman. He said that he had nearly taken a British ship single-handedly, with only an old iron nine-pound gun. Unfortunately, he said, the gun had burst apart as he fired the sixth round.

Then there was the adventure recalled by another old gentleman, who shall be nameless here. (He is too wealthy and respected a member of the community to be mentioned so lightly.) This fellow claimed that he'd had such excellent reflexes that, at the Battle of White Plains, he had deflected a musket ball with his sword! Yes, he said, he absolutely had felt the ball whiz around the blade of the sword and glance off at the hilt. To prove his claim, he was ready to show you the sword, pointing out where its hilt was a little bent.

Several more valiant citizens were present that night. To hear them tell it, all had been equally great on the battlefield, and each was eager to say that he had played a considerable part in bringing the war to a happy end.

However, all of these stories were nothing compared to the accounts of

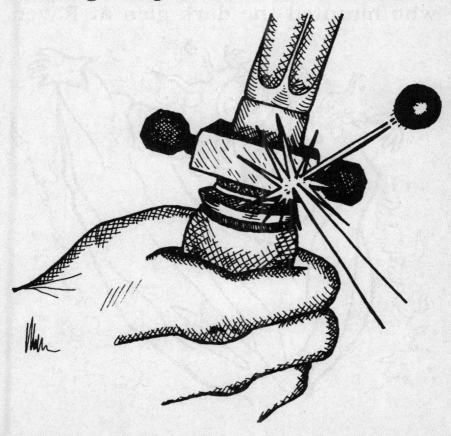

ghosts and apparitions that followed them. Several of the Sleepy Hollow people were present at Van Tassel's and, as usual, they were telling their wild and wonderful legends.

There were dark and gloomy tales about funeral trains. Several people described the strange cries of mourning heard near the great tree where the British spy, Major John André, had been captured. Some people mentioned the woman in white who haunted the dark glen at Raven

Rock. She had died in the snow there, and still could be heard shrieking on winter nights before a storm!

The main subject of the stories, however, was the favorite ghost of Sleepy Hollow, the Headless Horseman. He had been seen several times lately, patrolling the countryside or leading his horse among the graves in the yard of the old Dutch church.

The isolated location of the church seemed to make it a favorite haunt of troubled spirits. It stood on a little hill, surrounded by a grove of great elm trees. In the daylight, sunbeams shone down through the leaves to sleep quietly in the church's grass-grown yard. Seeing the church then, you might have thought that the dead would be able to rest in peace there.

On one side of the church there was a dark, secluded dell, which led into the thick woods. A large brook ran through it, among broken rocks and trunks of fallen trees. A small, wooden bridge stretched over a deep, black part of the stream. The bridge and the road that led to it were thickly shaded by overhanging trees. The shade cast a gloom over the place, even in the daytime. At night, the shadows became a fearful darkness.

The church bridge was one of the favorite haunts of the Headless Horseman, and the place where he was most often seen. The people of Sleepy Hollow

often told the tale of old Brouwer—a firm disbeliever in ghosts, they said. He was walking along a road one night, in another part of the valley, when the Horseman appeared. The ghost beckoned to Brouwer, and made him get up on the horse! The horse took off, galloping at breakneck speed over bushes and hills and swamps. Finally, they reached the church bridge. There, suddenly, the Horseman turned into a skeleton, threw

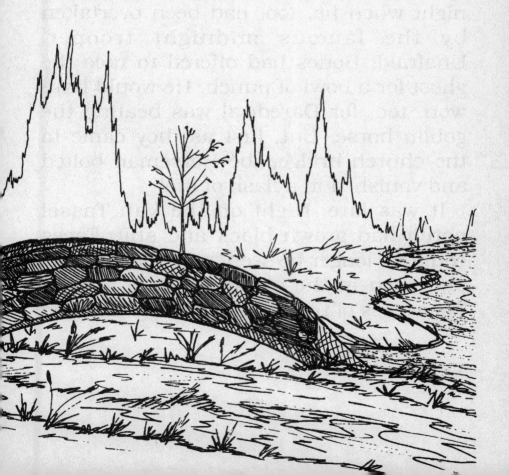

old Brouwer into the brook, and sprang away over the treetops with a clap of thunder!

Of course, someone told the story of old Brouwer that night on the Van Tassel porch. It was immediately matched by another story, from Brom Bones. The Headless Horseman wasn't such a great jockey after all, Brom claimed. Brom swore that he had been returning from the neighboring village of Sing Sing one night when he, too, had been overtaken by the famous midnight trooper. Unafraid, Bones had offered to race the ghost for a bowl of punch. He would have won, too, for Daredevil was beating the goblin horse. But, just as they came to the church bridge, the Horseman bolted and vanished in a flash of fire!

It was late. Night on the Van Tassel porch had grown black and still. Faces could no longer be seen, except every now and then in the small gleam of a pipe. The voices of the storytellers had dropped

into the hushed tones that people use in the dark. The chill of the night, and the great weight of many ghost stories, sank deep into Ichabod's bones.

About this time, the party broke up. The old farmers gathered their families in their wagons. They could be heard for some time, rattling along the roads and over the distant hills. In other wagons, young ladies sat on cushions behind their young men. Their lighthearted

laughter, mingling with the clatter of hooves, echoed among the silent woodlands. These echoes sounded fainter and fainter, until they gradually died away.

Finally, the scene of music and fun was silent and deserted. Only Ichabod lingered behind, according to the custom of country lovers, to have a heart-to-heart talk with Katrina. He did this with great confidence, fully convinced that he was now on the high road to success.

I will not pretend to know what exactly was said in this conversation. I am afraid, however, that something must have gone terribly wrong, for it was not too much later that Ichabod left the Van Tassel house with a heavy and desolate heart.

Oh, Katrina! Could she have been simply teasing Ichabod with her flirtatious tricks? Did she encourage the poor schoolteacher only as a game, to make Brom Bones jealous? Heaven only knows, not I!

In any case, Ichabod stole away from the Van Tassel house in a state of utter despair.

He did not look longingly at the magnificent farm, which he had all but owned in his imagination earlier that night. Instead, he went straight to the stable and, with several ill-tempered kicks and punches, jerked poor Gunpowder most rudely from his wonderful dreams of corn and oats and clover.

Chapter 5
The Midnight Ride of Ichabod Crane

It was the very witching time of night as Ichabod set out for home. The gloom of the hour matched his own. Far below him, the Tappan Zee spread its black waters. In the dead hush of midnight, he could hear the faint barking of a watchdog from the river's opposite shore. Elsewhere, something accidentally woke a rooster; its crowing came from far, far off, from a farmhouse away among the hills. It was like a dreaming sound in his ears.

There were few signs of life on the road near him. A lonely cricket chirped in the grass at the edge of the path. A grumpy bullfrog growled in a nearby marsh, as if it had been sleeping uncomfortably and turned suddenly in its bed.

All the stories of ghosts and goblins that Ichabod had heard in the evening came crowding in upon his mind. The night grew darker and darker. The stars seemed to sink deeper in the sky, and

driving clouds occasionally hid them from sight. Ichabod had never felt so lonely and dismal.

Also, he was approaching the scene where many of the ghost stories had been set. In the center of the road stood an enormous tulip tree, which towered like a giant above all the other trees. Its huge, gnarled limbs twisted nightmarishly almost down to the earth, then rose again into the air like human arms. Major André, a British spy, had been captured near that tree during the Revolutionary War. Because of that, the common people regarded it with great superstition. Many horrible spirits and cries of grief had been seen and heard there.

Ichabod began to whistle nervously as he drew close to the fearful tree. Another whistle answered back! No—it was only the wind sweeping sharply through the branches. Drawing a little nearer, he thought that he saw something white hanging in the midst of the tree. But on looking more closely, he saw that it was just a scar where the tree had been hit by lightning.

Suddenly, Ichabod heard a groan! His teeth chattered and his knees knocked furiously against the saddle. Again, it was only an innocent sound: one branch rubbing against another in the breeze.

Finally, he passed the tree in safety—but new perils lay before him.

Close to the tree, a small brook crossed

the road and ran into a thickly wooded marsh. A few rough logs, laid side by side, served as a bridge over the stream. A group of oak and chestnut trees, thickly matted with wild grapevines, threw a dark gloom over the place.

It was at this very spot that Major André had been seized. The men who captured him had hidden themselves in the thicket of vines. Ever since, the people of the area had considered the

stream haunted. Many a schoolboy had been terrified at having to pass this place alone after dark.

Ichabod's heart began to thump as he approached the stream, but it had to be crossed. The schoolmaster gathered up all his courage, gave his horse a half-dozen kicks in the ribs, and attempted to dash briskly across the bridge.

Instead of racing forward, however, the stubborn old animal made a sideways movement and ran up against a fence. Ichabod's right foot was trapped! The schoolmaster jerked the reins the other way and kicked furiously with his left foot. A lot of good that did him. The horse took off, but ran straight across the road, plunging straight into the bushes and thorns.

Ichabod panicked. He rained blows from both whip and heel on Gunpowder's scrawny old ribs. The horse finally dashed forward, snuffling and snorting. Then, suddenly, it came to a stop by the bridge—so quickly that Ichabod almost went sprawling over its head.

Just at this moment, a sound caught his ear. It was a splash, like the tramp of a horse's hoof in the water. Ichabod forced himself to look up. In the dark gloom of the grove, at the edge of the brook, he saw a towering black shadow. There was something there! The shadow did not move. It simply sat there in the darkness, like some gigantic monster ready to spring upon him!

The schoolmaster's hair rose upon his head with terror. What could he possibly do? It was too late to turn and run. If this was a ghost, how could he hope to escape a creature that could ride on the wings of the wind? Considering the situation, then, it took a lot of courage for Ichabod to stammer out a question to the figure.

"H-h-who are you?"

It did not reply.

Ichabod repeated his request: "H-who *are* you?"

Still there was no reply.

Once more, Ichabod tried to get away. He kicked his horse's sides furiously, but old Gunpowder refused to move. Poor Ichabod could think of nothing else to do, other than make a last-ditch appeal to Heaven. He shut his eyes and broke into a hymn, his voice shaking with fear and trembling.

Just then, the shadowy figure leaped over the brook and stood in the middle of the road. Ichabod could make out some of its shape in the darkness. It appeared to be a man of great height, mounted on a large and powerful black horse. Needless to say, the schoolteacher was not happy with this midnight companion— not with Brom Bones's story about the Headless Horseman burning in his overheated imagination.

Fortunately, old Gunpowder seemed to find his legs at last and began to move down the road. Ichabod spurred his steed to go faster, hoping to leave the stranger behind. The horseman quickened his horse to an equal pace. Ichabod tried slowing down to a walk, hoping that the other would pass him. But the stranger slowed down as well.

Ichabod's heart sank within him. He tried to sing his hymn again, but his tongue was completely dry and stuck to the roof of his mouth. He could not get out a note.

The stranger still had not said a word. This was frightening enough—but finding out why was worse.

The mysterious rider now reached a small rise in the road. Suddenly, he was outlined clearly against the sky. Looking back, Ichabod could see that he was gigantic in height, muffled in a cloak. Ichabod was horror-struck to see that the figure had no head! That is, there *was* a head, but it wasn't on the shoulders, where it should have been. Instead, the horseman carried his head in front of him, on the horn of his saddle!

Ichabod was no longer just terrified, he was desperate. He rained a shower of kicks and blows upon poor Gunpowder,

hoping to surprise the stranger and speed away quickly. But the ghost kept up with him. Away they galloped, stones flying and sparks flashing at every bound. Ichabod's flimsy clothes fluttered madly in the air in the frenzy of his flight.

Gunpowder was moving now! It was as if he was possessed by a demon. Without guidance from the schoolmaster, the

horse plunged headlong down a hill, taking a road that led through a sandy hollow. Ichabod recognized the way. They were headed for that place most famous in the Headless Horseman tales—the church bridge.

Unfortunately, just as they got halfway through the hollow, the straps on Gunpowder's saddle began to come

undone. Ichabod felt the saddle slipping from under him. He seized it by the horn and tried to hold on, but in vain. The schoolmaster had barely enough time to grasp the old horse around the neck before the saddle fell to the earth. A split second later, he heard it being trampled underfoot by the fearsome black horse.

The thought of Hans Van Ripper's anger passed through Ichabod's mind for just a moment. That was the old man's Sunday saddle, his best; he would be furious. But this was no time for petty fears. The goblin was hard on Ichabod's heels, and Ichabod had enough to do just to stay on the madly galloping horse. He kept nearly slipping off, sometimes falling to one side, sometimes to the other. Still other times, he flew up and came landing down on the high ridge of the horse's backbone so hard that he felt as if he would split in two!

Suddenly, the whitewashed wall of the old Dutch church appeared through the trees ahead. They were coming to the bridge. Ichabod remembered the stories about the Headless Horseman. It was at the bridge where he always disappeared. "If only I can reach that bridge, I will be safe," Ichabod thought.

Just then, he heard the black steed panting and blowing close behind him. He even thought that he could feel the horse's hot breath on his neck. Another mighty kick in Gunpowder's ribs—and now the old horse sprang up on the bridge, thundered over the wooden planks, and made it to the opposite side.

Ichabod cast a look over his shoulder to see if his pursuer would vanish in a flash of fire and brimstone. But the goblin was still there—closer than ever, rising in its stirrups, and in the very act of hurling its head at him!

Ichabod tried to dodge the horrible missile—but too late. It hit his own head with a tremendous crash. The school-teacher felt the blow, lost his grip, and

fell off the horse, tumbling headlong into the dust. In the blink of an eye, Gunpowder, and the black steed with the Headless Horseman riding it, passed by Ichabod Crane like a tornado.

Chapter 6
A New Mystery for Sleepy Hollow

The next morning, the old horse was found without its saddle, quietly eating the grass outside Van Ripper's gate. Ichabod did not appear at breakfast. The boys assembled at the schoolhouse, then strolled idly on the banks of the brook—without a schoolmaster. Dinner hour came. No Ichabod.

Hans Van Ripper finally began to worry about the fate of poor Ichabod, as well as his saddle. There was an investigation into the matter. After careful searching, people came upon traces of the schoolmaster. In one part of the road leading to the church, someone found Van Ripper's saddle. The horses' tracks, deeply imbedded in the saddle, were traced to the bridge. Beyond the bridge, on a bank of the brook, they found the hat of the unfortunate Ichabod and, close by the hat, a shattered pumpkin.

They searched the brook, but the body of the schoolmaster was not found. Hans Van Ripper, as executor of Ichabod Crane's estate, examined the bundle that contained all Ichabod's worldly possessions. It held two shirts, two stiff collars, two pairs of woolen socks, an old pair of corduroy pants, a rusty razor, a dog-eared hymn book, and a broken pitch pipe.

As for the books and furniture of the schoolhouse, they belonged to the community—all except Cotton Mather's *History of Witchcraft* and a book of

dreams and fortune-telling that were Ichabod's own. A piece of paper was found in the pages of the dream book. On it was a great deal of scribbling and crossing-out in the schoolmaster's handwriting—several fruitless attempts to write a poem for the heiress Katrina Van Tassel.

Without ceremony, Hans Van Ripper fed the magic books and the poetic scrawl to the flames of his fireplace. The old man

decided that, from that time forward, he would never send his children to school. "I never knew any good," he said, "to come of this reading and writing business."

Records showed that the schoolmaster had been paid a couple of days before he disappeared. Any money he had in the world must have been in his pockets that night.

The mysterious event caused much discussion and debate at the church on the following Sunday. Groups of gazers and gossipers were collected in the churchyard, at the bridge, and at the spot where the hat and pumpkin had been found. The stories of old Brouwer, of Bones, and of a host of others were called to mind. After the good church folk had seriously considered all the facts of the case—both the old stories and the current situation—they shook their heads and came to the same conclusion: Ichabod Crane had been carried off by the Headless Horseman.

Since Ichabod was a bachelor, had no family, and owed no money to anyone, nobody troubled his or her head anymore about him. The school was moved from that building to another one in a different spot in the hollow. Another schoolmaster soon reigned in Ichabod's spot.

It is true that an old farmer, who went down to New York City on a visit several years after, returned to say that Ichabod Crane was still alive. This man's story was

that the schoolmaster had fled from sheer fright—of the ghost as well as the saddle-less Hans Van Ripper. Perhaps Ichabod had also been a bit discouraged by the heiress Katrina Van Tassel. It was said that he had moved to a distant part of the country, where he had become a lawyer, turned politician, written for the news-papers, and finally was made a judge.

Then there was Brom Bones. Shortly after the disappearance of his rival,

Brom led the blooming Katrina in triumph to the marriage altar. Brom was seen to look especially smug whenever the story of Ichabod was told. He always burst into a hearty laugh at the mention of the pumpkin. This led some people to suspect that Brom knew more about that night than he chose to tell.

The old country wives, however, are the best judges of these matters. They insist, to this day, that Ichabod was spirited away by supernatural means. The story of Ichabod Crane and the Headless Horseman became a favorite story of theirs, and is often told around those winter evening fires that the schoolmaster himself had loved so well.

After this incident, the church bridge became, more than ever, a place of super-stitious awe. That may be the reason why the road has been changed in recent years, so that one can take a different route to reach the church.

The old, deserted schoolhouse soon

fell to decay. Many people would tell you that the building is haunted by the ghost of the unfortunate schoolmaster. It is not unusual, even now, for a boy to be wandering home on a still summer evening and to hear, at a distance, the voice of Ichabod Crane singing a melancholy hymn among the tranquil solitudes of Sleepy Hollow.

The End

Rip Van Winkle

Chapter 1
An Easygoing Fellow

**Found Among the Papers of
the Late Diedrich Knickerbocker.**

Anyone who has made a voyage up the Hudson River above Manhattan, New York, will remember the Catskill Mountains. Cousins of the great Appalachian family, they may be seen away to the west of the river, swelling up to a noble height.

At the foot of these mountains, the traveler may have seen chimney smoke curling up from a village whose shingle roofs gleam among the trees. It is quite an old village, founded by Dutch settlers in the days of their great leader, Peter Stuyvesant (may he rest in peace). Some of the houses of the original settlers still stand. They were built of small yellow bricks brought from Holland, with gable fronts and weathervanes on their roofs.

Many years ago, while this area was still a colony of England, there was a man

by the name of Rip Van Winkle who lived in one of those houses. He was a descendant of the Van Winkles who had fought so bravely with Peter Stuyvesant at the siege of Fort Christina. Our Rip had little of the military mind, however. He was a simple, quiet, good-natured fellow—a kind neighbor and an obedient husband.

Rip was also the kind of husband we call henpecked—that is, endlessly nagged by an unhappy wife. It is odd

that Dame Van Winkle was so cross with her husband all the time. Everyone else loved him. Rip was a great favorite with all the other wives of the village. They always took his side whenever they gossiped about the Van Winkles.

The children of the village, too, would shout with joy whenever he approached. He loved playing games and flying kites with them, and told them long stories of ghosts, witches, and Indians. A troop of children followed him wherever he went. They hung on his coat, climbed on his back, and played a thousand tricks on him. Rip accepted all this attention, even the tricks, with a laugh.

Even the *dogs* loved him. Not a single one would bark at him as he walked through the neighborhood!

There was one flaw in Rip's nature, which I should mention. It is true that he wasn't very good at making money for his family. I don't know why this was. He was certainly quite able to stick to a

task. Why, he could sit on a wet rock with a rod as long and heavy as a sword and fish *all day* without as much as a nibble. Also, he could go out hunting for hours at a time, carrying a heavy gun on his shoulder.

As for work, well, Rip never refused to assist a neighbor, even in the roughest of jobs. He was among the best in the countryside for husking corn. He was always there whenever a stone fence needed to

be built. The women of the village even used him to run the errands that their own husbands refused to do.

The problem was that Rip was ready to do anyone's work but his own. Working on other peoples' farms was easy. Keeping his own farm or family in order seemed to be impossible. It was a pretty sorry-looking farm, to be sure.

Rip's kids were also a sight. They looked as ragged and wild as if they belonged to nobody. Rip Jr., his son, was a chip off the old block. He seemed to have inherited his father's work habits. The boy was usually seen tripping at his mother's heels, dressed in his father's old hand-me-down pants. These were so big that he had to keep holding them up at the waist with one hand—like a lady does to keep the hem of her dress out of the mud.

Rip Van Winkle was just one of those happy humans who take the world easy. They can eat white bread or brown,

whichever takes less trouble. If left to himself, he would have whistled life away and been perfectly happy.

Unfortunately, Dame Van Winkle, his wife, kept chewing his ear off. Hour by hour, she scolded him for his idleness. "You're bringing ruin on the family!" she would wail. Morning, noon, and night, her tongue never stopped wagging. No matter what Rip said, she would shower him with abuse.

Rip had one way of replying to all her lectures, a way that had grown into a habit from frequent use. He would shrug his shoulders, shake his head slowly, cast his eyes upward, and say nothing. This would only set his wife into scolding again, so Rip would be forced to head outside—the only side of a house that belongs to a henpecked husband.

Rip's only ally at home was his dog, Wolf. Poor Wolf was as henpecked as his master. Dame Van Winkle considered the two of them to be companions in idleness. In the woods, Wolf was as brave a dog as any. But what courage can withstand the terrors of a harsh tongue? The moment Wolf entered the house, his head fell, his tail curled between his legs, and he sneaked through the rooms, trying not to be noticed. He kept Dame Van Winkle in the corner of his eye at all times. At the smallest wave of a broom handle or ladle, he was ready to fly to the door, yelping in terror.

Times grew worse and worse for Rip Van Winkle as the years rolled on. A bad temper never mellows with age, and a sharp tongue is the only tool that grows sharper from constant use.

Rip used to console himself in various ways. Often, he would walk down the street to join a group of other idle men of the village. This "club" held its "meetings" on a bench in front of an inn named for His Majesty, King George the Third of England, who still ruled America in those days. A portrait of the king was hung proudly on the front door.

The men loved to sit together in the shade through the length of a long, lazy, summer's day. They traded village gossip, or told endless sleepy stories about nothing. You should have heard the deep discussions that took place whenever someone found an old newspaper! How wisely they would discuss and explain some public event that had taken place months before!

Rip's main escape, however, was to take his gun and his dog and disappear into the woods. There he would sit at the foot of a tree and share his food with Wolf. "Poor Wolf," he would say. "You lead a dog's life because of my wife. But never mind. While I live, you will never lack a friend to stand by you." Wolf would wag his tail and look longingly at his master's face. If a dog can feel pity, Wolf certainly did.

Chapter 2
A Very
Strange Evening

On one such day, Rip wandered far, all the way to one of the highest parts of the Catskill Mountains. He had been squirrel hunting, and the quiet mountains had echoed and re-echoed with the sound of his gun.

Late in the afternoon, he sat down to rest on a grassy hill overlooking the valley. He looked at the beautiful Hudson River far, far below him, moving on its silent, majestic course. The sun was setting. The mountains had begun to throw their long blue shadows over the valleys. Rip saw that it would be dark before he could reach the village. He heaved a heavy sigh when he thought of his wife. Oh, the terrors he would face when he got home late!

Rip had started down the mountain for home when, suddenly, he heard a voice from a distance. "Rip Van Winkle! Rip Van Winkle!" it called. He looked around, but saw nothing except a crow flying through the sky. He thought that he must have imagined it. But then the voice came again. "Rip Van Winkle! Rip Van Winkle!"

Rip looked anxiously in the direction of the voice. Finally, a figure appeared. It was a man walking slowly up the hill, carrying a heavy load on his back. Rip was surprised to see any human being in this place. But the man knew his name! Thinking that the man must be a neighbor of his, Rip ran down to help him.

Rip found, however, that this was no

neighbor. He was surprised at the odd-
ness of the man's appearance. He was a
short, stocky old fellow with thick,
bushy hair and a graying beard. He was
dressed in the old Dutch way, with an
old-fashioned vest and a pair of pants
decorated with rows of buttons down the
sides. The man carried a heavy-looking
barrel. He motioned for Rip to come and
help him with it.

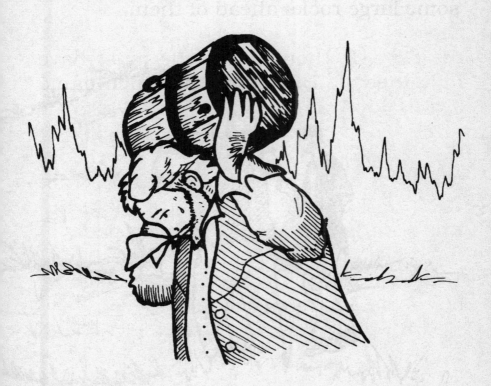

Rip was naturally puzzled, and a little distrustful. But he was a man who always helped out—he couldn't help himself. So he went to help the odd man carry the barrel. The two of them walked slowly up a narrow gully that looked like a dry river bed. Every now and then, Rip could hear long, echoing sounds, like peals of distant thunder. These seemed to come from a deep ravine between some large rocks ahead of them.

The two men walked in silence, even though Rip was full of questions. Why would this odd fellow be carrying a heavy barrel at the top of this mountain, so far from any town?

In time, Rip and the stranger came to the ravine and passed between the rocks. There, before them, was a field. On that field stood a bunch of other men who looked just as odd as Rip's companion, and these odd-looking men were bowling!

What a strange sight. The men were dressed in the old Dutch style, as I have said. Their faces were just as odd as their clothes. One had broad cheeks but small, piggish eyes. Another had a huge nose that was almost as big as the rest of his face. This fellow was wearing a white hat shaped like a sugarloaf with a little red rooster's tail on top. All the men had beards, of various shapes and colors.

One of the men seemed to be the leader. He was a stout old gentleman with a weatherbeaten face, who wore a tall hat with a feather and high-heeled shoes with roses in the buckles. The whole group reminded Rip of one of those old Flemish paintings that Baltus Van Tassel and the village parson had brought over from Holland.

Another odd thing: The men were playing a game, yet they frowned as if something awful were happening. They were having the saddest bit of fun that Rip had ever seen. They played in absolute

silence. The only sound was the noise of the rolling balls, which sent a long echo among the mountains. That sound was the thunder that Rip had heard!

The odd men stopped their game as Rip and his companion approached. Suddenly, Rip found the whole group of strange faces staring at him with fierce expressions. They looked like a bunch of menacing statues. It was an eerie sight, I can tell you. Rip's heart trembled and his knees knocked together.

The first odd man now began pouring a liquid that looked something like beer from the barrel into large flagons—tall, old-fashioned glasses. He made a sign for Rip to wait where he was. Rip obeyed with fear and trembling. The group of odd fellows drank in a profound silence, and then returned to their game.

In time, Rip grew less afraid. After all, the odd men did not seem dangerous. When no one was looking, Rip even dared to take a sip from his flagon. It

was pretty good, whatever it was, so he
had another flagon full. It got better.
One taste inspired the next one, which
inspired the one after that, and so on.

Rip made many visits to the barrel. Eventually, a fog settled on his brain. His eyes swam in his head. Rip sat heavily at the base of a tree. His head nodded on his chest, and he fell into a deep sleep.

Chapter 3
An Even Stranger Morning

When Rip awoke, he found himself back on the grassy hill where he had first seen the odd man. He rubbed his eyes. It was a bright, sunny morning. The birds were hopping and twittering among the bushes. An eagle was wheeling high above, coasting on the pure mountain breeze. "Surely, I have not slept here all night," Rip thought.

Yet it seemed that he had. Rip recalled the events of the previous evening: the strange man with the keg, the mountain ravine, the miserable-looking party of odd fellows bowling, and the flagon. "Oh, that flagon! That wicked flagon," thought Rip. "What excuse can I make to Dame Van Winkle?" Also, how had he ever ended up back on that grassy hill?

Rip looked around for his gun. In the grass beside him lay a rusted old firearm. Its lock had fallen off and other parts of it were eaten away by age. "This can't be mine!" he thought—not the gun that he cleaned and oiled every day. "It was those men," Rip said to himself. "Those bowlers must have waited till I fell asleep, then stole my gun!"

Then came another thought: Where was Wolf? "Maybe he wandered off after a squirrel or a partridge," Rip thought. He whistled and shouted for his dog. The name echoed around the mountainside, but no Wolf appeared.

Rip decided to return to the scene of the bowling party and demand the

return of his dog and gun. As he rose to
his feet, he found himself terribly stiff in
the joints. "These mountain beds do not
agree with me," he thought. "If I wind up
with aches and pains from this, I will
have a devil of a time with my wife."

He retraced his steps from the evening before and found the ravine. To his surprise, there was a roaring mountain stream tumbling from between the rocks. Just the day before, there had been nothing there but a dry creek bed! Rip fought his way through brambles

and grapevines—which had also grown up, magically, overnight—to the spot where the men had been bowling. The field was filled with rushing water.

Again he called and whistled after his dog. The only answer came from the caw-ing of a flock of idle crows, sitting in a

tree high above him. They seemed to look down and laugh at his terrible confusion.

What was to be done? The morning was passing away, and Rip was very hungry. He grieved to give up his dog and gun and dreaded facing his wife, but it wouldn't be good to starve to death in the mountains, either. So Rip shook his head, put the rusty firearm on his shoulder, and started homeward with a heart full of trouble and worry.

As he approached the village, he met a number of people but didn't recognize any of them. This was strange; he thought he knew everyone in these parts. The way they dressed was slightly odd, too. The people he met stared at Rip with equal surprise and kept stroking their chins. What did this mean? Rip touched his own chin and found, to his shock, that his beard had grown a foot long!

Rip finally came to the village. A troop of strange children ran at his heels, hoot-

ing after him and pointing at his long,
gray beard. The dogs were all strangers,
too, and they barked at him. The village
had changed, as well—it was larger and
more crowded. Rows of new houses had
appeared and favorite places were gone.
Signs with strange names on them hung
over the doors, and strange faces gazed
out the windows. Everything was strange.

"Is this the work of some kind of
witch?" Rip asked himself in wonder. He

was very anxious. "Whatever was in that flagon last night has confused my poor head terribly," he thought.

Because there were so many new houses, it took some time for Rip to find his own. He approached it cautiously, expecting to hear the shrill voice of Dame Van Winkle at any moment.

The sight of the house filled him with alarm. It was all decayed! The roof had fallen in, the windows were shattered, and the doors were off their hinges. A half-starved dog that *looked* like Wolf snarled at him. "My very own dog has forgotten me!" Rip sighed.

The inside of the house was even more troubling. It was empty, forlorn, and seemed to have been abandoned. The sight of it caused Rip to forget all his fear of punishment. He called loudly for his wife and children. The lonely rooms rang for a moment with his voice, then all was silent again.

Rip hurried to his old refuge, the village

inn. It, too, was gone! In its place stood a larger building, no longer named after King George. The Union Hotel was the name on the sign. The great tree that had stood in front of the inn was also gone. Instead, there was a tall flagpole. A flag that Rip had never seen before flew at the top of the pole—an odd collection of stars and stripes!

There was one thing that Rip recognized—the painting of King George on the sign of the village inn. But even *this* had been changed. The king's red coat was now blue, he held a sword instead of a royal scepter, and his head was topped by a three-cornered hat. Underneath the king's portrait, the words *General Washington* were painted in large letters.

A large crowd of folks bustled about the door of the inn: Something was going on. Rip didn't see a single familiar face. He looked in vain for one of his old comrades, who might be reading aloud the contents

of some ancient newspaper. Instead, there was an unpleasant-looking fellow, his pockets full of handbills, who was shouting in an obnoxious way about many strange things. He threw about such phrases as "the rights of citizens," "elections," "members of Congress," "liberty," "Bunker Hill," "the heroes of 1776"—terms that Rip had never heard before. What was this man shouting about? Rip wondered. It was almost a foreign language to him.

Rip's appearance soon caught the attention of the crowd there. He must have been a strange sight, with his long beard, shabby clothes, rusty gun, and the army of children at his feet. The people at the inn crowded around him, looking him up and down. The loud man with the handbills rushed up to him. "Which side did you vote on?" he loudly demanded. "Which party are you with?"

Rip was dumbfounded. He had no idea what the man was talking about.

Another man in a sharp cocked hat

broke away from the group and planted himself before Rip in a self-important way. Putting his hands on his hips, he looked sternly into Rip's eyes as if he were able to look into his very soul.

"What brings you to this election, sir, with a gun on your shoulder and a mob at your heels?" he demanded. The man seemed angry! "Do you mean to start a riot in the village?"

"Alas, gentlemen," Rip cried with dismay, "I am a poor, quiet man, a native of this village, and a loyal subject of the King, God bless him."

The place exploded with shouting. "A spy! An English spy! Away with him!" They looked as if they were ready to swarm over poor Rip. The self-important man in the cocked hat held up his hands and finally restored order in the unruly crowd. Then he turned back to Rip with an expression even more stern. "Who are you, sir?" he demanded. "Why have you come here? Who are you seeking?"

"I assure you, I mean no harm," poor Rip said, his voice shaking. "I merely come in search of some of my friends, who gather at this inn."

"Well, who are they, then? Name them," the man said.

"Where's Nicholas Vedder?" Rip asked.

There was silence for a moment, then an old man spoke up. "Nicholas Vedder? Why, he is dead and gone eighteen years now! There is a wooden tombstone in the churchyard that used to tell all about him, but most of it has rotted away."

Confused and saddened, Rip tried another name. "Where's Brom Dutcher?"

"Oh, he went off to the army in the beginning of the war," said the old man. "Some folks say that he was killed at the battle of Stony Point. Others say that he was drowned in a storm offshore. I don't know; he never came back again."

"Then where's Van Brummel, the schoolmaster?" Rip asked.

"He went off to the war, too," someone else answered. "Van Brummel was a great general, and is now in Congress."

Rip's heart sank, hearing of all these strange changes. Was he all alone in the world, then? Every answer to his questions puzzled him. It seemed as if a very long period of time had passed. The people kept speaking of matters that he did not understand: war, Congress, Stony Point. Rip did not have the courage to ask about other friends. Instead, he cried out in despair, "Does nobody here know Rip Van Winkle?"

"Oh, Rip Van Winkle!" two or three of them exclaimed. "Oh, to be sure. There is Rip Van Winkle over there, leaning against that tree."

Rip looked—and beheld an exact copy of himself, just as he had looked the day he went up the mountain! Certainly, this fellow seemed just as lazy and ragged.

Poor Rip was now completely confused. He doubted his own identity. Was he himself or someone else?

Just then, the man in the cocked hat demanded to know who he was.

"God knows," Rip said, at his wit's end. "I'm not myself; I'm somebody else. That's me over there—no, that's somebody else in my shoes. I was myself last night, but I fell asleep on the mountain. Now they've changed my gun, and everything's changed, and I'm changed, and I can't tell what my name is or who I am."

The people now began to look at each other, nod, wink, and tap their fingers against the sides of their heads. They began to whisper about getting that gun away from the old fellow before he got himself into trouble.

At this moment, a young mother pressed through the crowd to get a good look at him. She had a child in her arms; the child was frightened by the sight of the old man and started to cry.

"Hush, Rip," said the mother to her child. "Hush; the old man won't hurt you." The name of the child and the mother's voice awakened a memory in the man with the long, gray beard.

"What is your name, my good woman?" he asked.

"Judith Gardener."

"And your father's name?"

"Ah, poor man, his name was Rip Van Winkle. Twenty years ago, he went away from home with his gun and has not been heard from since. His dog came home without him. Nobody knows if he fell down the mountain, shot himself accidentally, or was carried away by Indians. I was just a little girl then."

Rip had only one more question, which he asked in a faltering voice. "Where is your mother?"

"Oh, she is dead, too," said Judith Gardener. "She broke a blood vessel in her neck while screaming at a salesman who came to the door."

Rip could no longer stop himself. He took his daughter and her child in his arms. "I am your father!" he cried. "Young Rip Van Winkle once, old Rip Van Winkle now. Does nobody recognize poor Rip Van Winkle?"

Everyone stood amazed. There was a stunned silence. Finally, an old woman emerged from the crowd, put her hand

to her brow, and stared into Rip's face. "Sure enough!" she said. "It is Rip Van Winkle himself. Welcome home again, old neighbor. Where have you been for twenty long years?"

Rip's story was soon told, for the whole twenty years was only one night to him. The neighbors stared when they heard it. Some winked at each other, or rolled their eyes, or put their tongues in their cheeks. The self-important man in the cocked hat apparently did not believe it at all. He screwed down the corners of his mouth and shook his head. Seeing him, a number of people did the same. There was a lot of head shaking in that crowd.

But then old Peter Vanderdonk, great-grandson of the famous historian, was seen coming slowly up the road. The people decided to ask his opinion. Peter was the most ancient citizen of the village, and knew all the stories and legends of the area. He remembered Rip at once. Even better, he believed Rip's story of the strange old Dutchmen bowling. It was a fact, he said, that the Catskill Mountains were haunted by strange beings. The great Henry Hudson himself had returned there once every twenty years with the crew of his ship, the *Half Moon*, to keep watch over the river called by his name. "My own father," said Peter, "had seen the old men on that mountain bowling—and we've all heard those peals of thunder, haven't we?"

Chapter 4
A New World

To make a long story short, the group broke up and returned to the more important concerns of the election. Old Rip's daughter took him home to live with her. She had a snug, well-furnished house, and a cheery husband—whom Rip remembered as one of the boys who used to crawl on his back. Rip's son, the double image of the old man, was put to work on the farm. Unfortunately, he was his father's son when it came to labor.

Rip went back to his old walks and habits. He soon found many of his former friends. They all showed the wear and tear of time, I'm afraid. Rip came to prefer making friends among the young people, and they enjoyed his company.

Rip had arrived at that age when it is okay to do absolutely nothing. He took his place once more on the bench by the inn door, where he was considered one of the village elders. People also looked to Rip as someone who could speak of those old times "before the war."

It took a while for him to understand the important events that he had slept through. There had been a revolution, a war by which the country had thrown off the yoke of the British and King George. They now were all free citizens of a new country, called the United States. That was fine with Rip—he was no politician. The changes of countries and empires didn't bother him much. There was only one freedom from harsh rule that meant

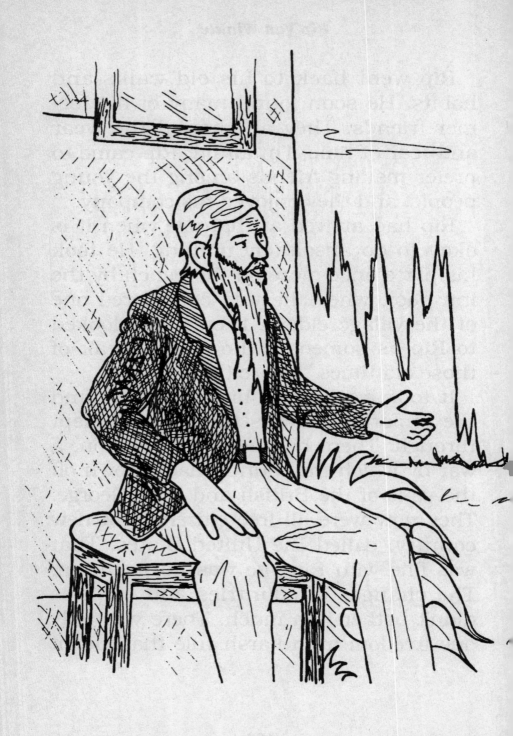

anything to him, and that was the freedom from the harsh rule of his wife!

He now had that freedom. Dame Van
Winkle was gone, so Rip could come and
go as he pleased. Whenever her name
was mentioned, he had the same expression. He would shake his head, shrug
his shoulders, and cast his eyes up to
Heaven. People read this as a sign that

Rip had come to accept his sad fate as a widowed man. Of course, it might have meant that he was happy to be free.

Rip told his story to every stranger who arrived at the inn. In time, there was not a man, woman, or child in the area who didn't know it by heart. There were always some people who doubted it, and said that Rip was crazy.

The old Dutch people of the town, however, believed every word of his story. To this day, whenever they hear thunder on a summer afternoon in the Catskill Mountains, they say, "There's old Henry Hudson and his crew bowling again." Troubled hearts of the area remember the story, too, whenever life hangs heavy on their hands. They wish for nothing less than to have a calming drink from that mysterious flagon of Rip Van Winkle's.

The End

ABOUT THE AUTHOR

WASHINGTON IRVING was born in New York, New York, on April 3, 1783. He was the pampered youngest of eleven children. While studying to become a lawyer, he wrote light-hearted essays that poked fun at New York society.

In 1806, he began practicing law, but kept writing. In 1809, under the pen name of Diedrich Knickerbocker, he published a humorous book called *A History of New York*. He went on to publish other popular books, including *The Sketch Book of Geoffrey Crayon*. Among the stories in that book were his two most well-known, "The Legend of Sleepy Hollow" and "Rip Van Winkle." Called the first American short stories, they were as loved in his time as they remain today.

Irving continued to write, but also served the U.S. government as a diplomat in Spain. He died in Tarrytown, New York, on November 28, 1859.

The Young Collector's
Illustrated Classics®

The Adventures of Huckleberry Finn
The Adventures of Robin Hood
The Adventures of Sherlock Holmes
The Adventures of Tom Sawyer
Anne of Green Gables
Black Beauty
Call of the Wild
Dracula
Frankenstein
Gulliver's Travels
Heidi
The Hunchback of Notre Dame
Jane Eyre
The Legend of Sleepy Hollow & Rip Van Winkle
A Little Princess
Little Women
Moby Dick
Oliver Twist
Peter Pan
The Prince and the Pauper
Rebecca of Sunnybrook Farm
The Red Badge of Courage
Robinson Crusoe
The Secret Garden
The Strange Case of Dr. Jekyll and Mr. Hyde
Swiss Family Robinson
Tales of Terror and Suspense
The Time Machine
Treasure Island
20,000 Leagues Under the Sea
The War of the Worlds
White Fang

These Illustrated Classics are available for special
and educational sales from:
www.kidsbooks.com

Kidsbooks, Inc.
230 Fifth Avenue
New York, NY 10001
(212) 685-4444